HOT WHEELS™

To the Extreme

By Benjamin Harper
Illustrated by Ed Wisinski and Dave White

SCHOLASTIC INC.
New York Toronto London Auckland Sydney
Mexico City New Delhi Hong Kong Buenos Aires

For information regarding permission, write to Scholastic Inc., Attention: Permissions Department, 557 Broadway, New York, NY 10012.

ISBN-13: 978-0-545-02019-0
ISBN-10: 0-545-02019-0

12 11 10 9 8 7 6 5 4 3 2 1   7 8 9 10 11/0

Printed in the U.S.A.
First printing, November 2007

Building your own car can be exciting.

Some people like simple cars.

Other people like to
make their cars extreme.

This ice-cream truck is ready to go.
Two scoops, please!

It delivers cones at top speed.

This car is as big as a tank.

The spoiler on the back
helps it go fast.

Zoom! Around the track it goes!

Look! It is another racer.
It is going very fast.

Whoosh! The car
races like a rocket.

Its tail makes it super speedy.

The tires on this car are big.

This car is ready for action!

Four-wheeling is exciting!

The driver likes to take this car off the road.

That was a bumpy ride!

This ride is smooth and fast.

This car is as sleek as a spaceship.
It looks like it could fly!

The engine is on the outside.

The engine on this car is enormous.
Vroom! It is really loud, too.

Six wheels make this car powerful.

Look out! Those back wheels are huge!

These cars can drive
over mud and rocks.

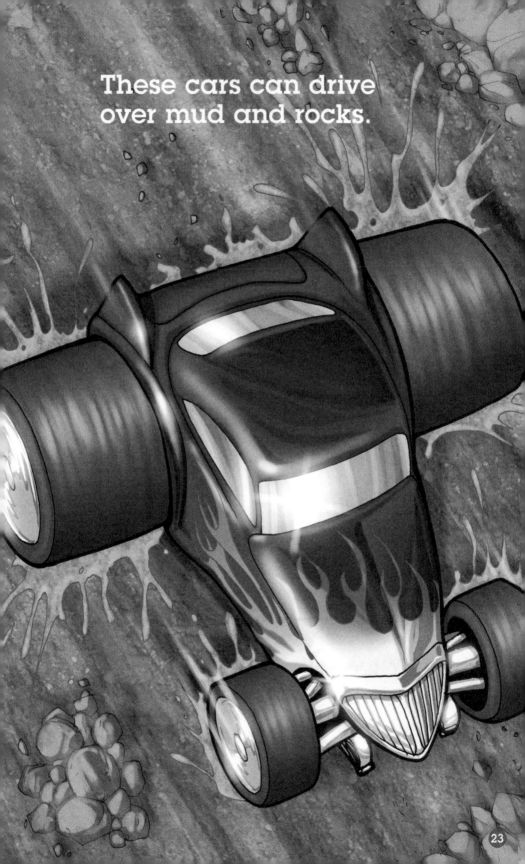

These racers ride low
to the ground.

The green car flies
past the other cars
on the track.

The doors on this car
are made of wood.

It may look old-fashioned,
but it is still fast.

Not all extreme vehicles are cars.

This motorcycle soars
by at top speeds.

It is exciting to take things to the extreme!